Scholastic

A READING GUIDE TO

Julie of the Wolves

by Jean Craighead George

Danielle Denega

Copyright © 2004 by Scholastic Inc.
Interview © 2004 by Jean Craighead George

All rights reserved. Published by Scholastic Inc.

SCHOLASTIC, SCHOLASTIC REFERENCE, SCHOLASTIC BOOKFILES, and associated logos are trademarks and/or registered trademarks of Scholastic Inc.

No part of this publication may be reproduced, or stored in a retrieval system, or transmitted in any form or by any means, electronic, mechanical, photocopying, recording, or otherwise, without written permission of the publisher. For information regarding permission, write to Scholastic Inc., Attention: Permissions Department, 557 Broadway, New York, NY 10012.

Library of Congress Cataloging-in-Publication Data

Scholastic BookFiles: A reading guide to Julie of the wolves by Jean Craighead George/Danielle Denega.   p. cm.

Summary: Discusses the writing, characters, plot, and themes of this 1972 novel. Includes discussion questions and activities. Includes bibliographical references (p.).

1. George, Jean Craighead, 1919– . Julie of the Wolves— Juvenile literature.   2. Arctic regions—In literature—Juvenile literature.   3. Eskimos in literature—Juvenile literature. 4. Wolves in literature—Juvenile literature   [1. George, Jean Craighead, 1919– . Julie of the Wolves.   2. American literature— History and criticism.]   I. Title.   II. Series.

PS3557.E485J854   2004

813′.54—dc21   2003042842

0-439-53835-1

10 9 8 7 6 5 4 3 2 1   04 05 06 07 08

Composition by Brad Walrod/High Text Graphics, Inc.
Cover and interior design by Red Herring Design

Printed in the U.S.A.   23
First printing, March 2004

Contents

"I had much to paint and write about."

—Jean Craighead George

From a very early age, Jean Craighead George was very ambitious. She remembers being six years old and deciding that she would be not only a writer, but also an illustrator, a dancer, a poet, and a mother. Did she follow *all* of these dreams? She did—and then some! She began writing in the third grade, and hasn't stopped since. She has written more than one hundred books.

Jean Craighead was born on July 2, 1919, in Washington, D.C. Her dad, Frank C. Craighead, was an entomologist (a scientist who studies insects) and a botanist (a scientist who studies plants). Her mother, Mary, and her brothers, aunts, and uncles were also students of nature. Jean and her older twin brothers, John and Frank, grew up spending their summers in the wilderness along the Potomac River.

It was during these summers that Jean says her father taught her about trees, flowers, birds, and insects, and even how to find and harvest wild foods. Jean was always drawn to the outdoors. She liked to fish, play softball, swim, catch frogs, and ride around in hay wagons with her brothers. Jean Craighead read lots of classic literature and kept journals of what she saw and learned during her summers along the river with her family. She developed a sense of respect for nature and the earth. "I had much to paint and write about," she has said.

Jean Craighead went to college at Pennsylvania State University, where she earned degrees in science and literature. After college, she was a reporter for the The Washington Post newspaper and worked for the White House Press Corps as a reporter covering news at the White House. She found journalism exciting and says: "I met senators, diplomats and the President of the United States, Franklin Delano Roosevelt." She got married in 1944 to John Lothar George, who was the college roommate of one of her brothers. Her name then became Jean Craighead George. John was in the Navy at the time, serving in World War II. After the war ended, Jean and John went to Michigan so that John could attend the University of Michigan and earn his doctorate (PhD). They both wanted to understand nature better, so the two lived in a tent in a maple forest while they were there. Jean says, "It was here that I truly came to understand the beauty and complexity of the natural world."

At first, Jean wrote books with her husband. The first one, *Vulpes the Red Fox*, came out in 1948. The two wrote this and several more animal biographies together. They based the books on real-life experiences they had with animals they took in from the wild and kept as pets. Their writing partnership was very successful. In fact, they even won an award for best nature writing for their book *Dipper of Copper Creek*.

Jean was very excited to become a mother. The first child she and John had was a daughter, whom they named Carolyn Laura but call Twig, because she was so tiny. The Georges moved to Poughkeepsie, New York, just north of New York City. Two years later, they had a son, John Craighead, whom they call Craig. Four years after that, John and Jean had another son, Thomas Luke, whom they call Luke.

Jean loves being a mother. When her kids were young, she brought wild animals into the house for them to learn about. First Jean wrote about the animals themselves, and then about her children interacting with the animals. "I kept on writing and illustrating, for this is what I did well because I loved it."

In 1957, the family moved to neighboring Chappaqua, New York, when John took a job working at the Bronx Zoo. Jean continued her writing. She gained the greatest recognition when she began writing books on her own. In 1959, *My Side of the Mountain* was published. This is one of Jean Craighead George's best-known books. It is a survival story about a boy named Sam Gribley. She based the story on her childhood experiences with her father and twin brothers. It was written as her own children napped and slept at night.

In 1964, Jean and John divorced. Jean stayed in Chappaqua and continued to write. She wrote articles for *Reader's Digest* and continued to write books for both children and adults. She traveled across America with her children, taking them to places where they could study animals and plants. They climbed mountains together, hiked deserts, and went canoeing on rivers.

Her observations while on these trips became material for her books.

It was after a trip to Alaska in 1970 with her youngest child, Luke, that Jean returned home and wrote *Julie of the Wolves*. The book tells the story of a brave Eskimo girl who gets lost on the Alaskan tundra while running away from home. The heroine forms a close bond with wild wolves. They help her survive. The book was published in 1972, and in 1973, it received the John Newbery Medal. This honor is given to the author of the most distinguished piece of children's literature from the previous year. Just a few years after it was published, *Julie of the Wolves* was picked by the Children's Literature Association as one of the 10 best American children's books in the past 200 years.

Jean Craighead George's children are grown now, but they share their mother's love of nature and writing. They all went to college, and now Twig is a children's-book writer, just like her mom. Craig studies whales in Alaska and writes articles for scientific journals. Luke is a college professor in California and also writes articles for scientific journals. George says, "We are all deeply connected by our early love of the outdoors."

Jean Craighead George still lives in Chappaqua, New York, where she enjoys spending time reading to her five grandchildren when they visit. She still travels once a year with her family. They go to places like Maine, Hawaii, the rain forests of Belize, or to see the coral reefs in the Caribbean. She still writes books and is actively involved in trying to get new environmental protection bills passed through Congress.

> "I love their devotion to each other.
> They stay together partly for
> economic reasons, but mainly because
> of their deep affection and loyalty."
>
> —Jean Craighead George, on wolves

Before writing *Julie of the Wolves*, Jean Craighead George first researched wolf behavior. She read about them and learned that wolves are friendly and form well-run societies, like people do. Wolves communicate with one another using a combination of sight, sound, scent, color, and posture. This excited Jean and she wanted to learn more.

In 1970, she took her youngest son, Luke, on a trip to Alaska. She went because she was writing an article for *Reader's Digest* on wolves. They went to the Arctic Research Laboratory in the city of Barrow. Jean and Luke spent time doing professional research with the scientists at the laboratory.

The scientists observed the *Canis lupus*, which are gray wolves. From these scientists Jean learned about wolf communication firsthand. She was taught to give wolves a submissive grin, how to grunt-whine to get their attention in a friendly way, and to say hello to them by smiling with her mouth open. Jean became aware that wild wolves will approach a human who is on hands and knees but not one who is standing. She also learned about the mated pair of dominant wolves, called alphas, in each pack.

After studying with the scientists for a while, Jean and Luke went to Denali State Park in Alaska, where they lay on their bellies and observed wolves in their natural environment. George encountered a magnificent alpha-male wolf while she was there. He was the leader of a pack that lived in the state park.

Jean and Luke also noticed some people in Alaska who made an impression on them. When the two flew into Barrow, Luke happened to see a young Eskimo girl out on the tundra and remarked that she was "awfully little to be out there alone." Later on in their trip, Jean and Luke actually found themselves lost for a little while. They couldn't find their way on the flat tundra, which had no landmarks to guide them.

It was also on this trip that George met the woman on whom she based Miyax's (Julie's) character. She says, "A woman named Julia Sebevan took me in and told me about the old ways of the Eskimos." George still treasures a parka that Julia made for her, baleen (a portion of a whale's jaw) given to her by Julia's son, and, most of all, the relationship she formed with this woman and her family.

The alpha-male wolf, the little girl wandering the tundra alone, and Julia Sebevan all stayed in Jean's memories for a long time after she and Luke returned home. She says, "They haunted me for a year or more, as did the words of one of the scientists at the lab." The scientist told her that he no longer felt there was any doubt that a man could live with the wolves. He said that wolves are highly social and affectionate.

She decided to create a book using all she had learned about the tundra (its harsh climate and conditions), the wolves (from the scientists in Barrow and on her own), and the Eskimo people. She had no idea that *Julie of the Wolves* would become an award-winning book when she set out to write it. In fact, she says, "I thought I'd be severely criticized because it dealt with communication between man and wolf. At that time, the first experiments were just being run on animal communication. I didn't think an audience would tolerate it. But they did. They loved it."

An Interview with Jean Craighead George

◆ *When you left* Julie of the Wolves *open-ended, what did you hope readers would imagine Julie did next?*

The final sentence, "Julie pointed her boots toward Kapugen," is an Eskimo ending, meaning that it is open-ended with a big clue as to what is next. I changed Julie's name from the Eskimo Miyax, which I call her while she is on the tundra with the wolves, to Julie, which is her American/Western culture name. That in itself is an ending. I hope the readers will understand that Julie went home to her father, knowing he is not perfect but loving him anyway and that she is going to try to adapt to the new world of change that has come to the Eskimo.

◆ *Why did you write sequels to* Julie of the Wolves?

Long ago students and readers asked me to write more about Julie, but I felt I did not know enough about the Eskimo culture until my son, Craig, moved to Barrow, Alaska, to study the bowhead whale. He settled down there. For years I visited him and his family (I still do) and came to know his wonderful native friends. Twenty-one years later, I felt ready to write the sequel to *Julie of the Wolves*—and I did. That book is *Julie*. As for *Julie's*

Wolf Pack (third in the trilogy), I would have written that book sooner, but the relationship of the wolves in a pack was only guesswork. Then came [a greater understanding of] DNA and Dr. L. David Mech, [who] sampled almost a dozen Arctic [wolf] packs and found the truth. The alphas are strangers who meet and mate. The first pups spend the year learning from their parents and stay on to help with the next litter of pups. The aunts and uncles take positions in the pack according to their talents—some are good hunters, some swift runners. When a pack needs a wolf to replace a lost member, the alphas will "invite" one into the pack. A wolf pack is a very nice society.

◆ *How involved have you been in the creation of the movie,* Julie of the Wolves? *When is it being released?*

The movie is on hold. The screenplay was getting too far from the book, and so I did not sign the option [part of a contract] when it ran out. Someone will do it right. At present, a musical [theater] version of *Julie of the Wolves* is in the workshop stage of development and is breathtaking it is so beautiful.

◆ *If you found yourself in a situation similar to Julie's, do you think you would have managed as well as she did?*

I certainly would not have managed as well as Julie did in the same situation. Although my father, like Julie's father, taught me to hunt and fish and find delicious wild plants in the Eastern forests, I did not have the cultural sense of survival that Julie had. I could have made it for a few days in my Eastern woods, but since Dad taught me to follow a stream when lost because it leads to people, I would have been down that stream and out of the woods in a short time.

♦ *What would you say is the most important message you convey to readers in* Julie of the Wolves?

I hope that the message I conveyed in *Julie of the Wolves* is to tell young people to think things out. Think independently.

♦ *What is your writing process? When and how do you write? Can you describe a typical day (setting, time of day, etc.)?*

My writing process is a mix of research, personal experiences, washing the dishes, raising kids while thinking—then writing. I get up about five or five thirty [in the morning], shower, have breakfast and do all those personal things—even answer e-mail. Then I sit down at the computer and write. By this time I have done all the footwork—studied an animal, talked to scientists who are experts, camped in the area I am writing about to learn the ecology, and thought out a story. I think up the story when I am cooking or vacuuming the house or doing other jobs that don't take much mental work. Sometimes the animal I am writing about has done something that makes a story and sometimes it is a young boy or girl who is the secret. I do like to put kids in my nature books because as a lovely Eskimo woman said to me, "People are nature, too." Around three o'clock I give up, go swimming, find a friend, or call one of my three children and five grandchildren and listen to their adventures. Grandson Luke went camping on the tundra (he lives in Barrow, Alaska), granddaughter Caity (Maryland) wrote a short story about the mall. Grandson Hunter (California) fed a raven cheese.

◆ *What type of writing do you find the toughest? the easiest?*

The hardest writing is when I don't know enough about a subject to "let it flow." The easiest for me is telling a story. I love to tell stories.

◆ *If you weren't a writer, what might you be?*

. . . I suppose I could paint houses for a living, or deliver newspapers, but I have wanted to be a writer since I was in third grade and haven't developed any other skills. My thoughts then were that if I wasn't good enough to be a writer, I could dance, canoe, paint pictures, be a politician, or help a librarian put books back on the shelves. But I never perfected any of those desires, so it is fortunate that I stuck to my love.

◆ *Do you have any advice for young aspiring writers?*

My advice to young writers is to write, write, write and read, read, read. Then go out in the world and listen and observe. Writing even a line or two every day will help you attain the discipline that is needed to write. And, if you don't truly love every minute of it, try something else.

◆ *When you're not writing, what do you enjoy doing?*

When I am not writing I enjoy hiking, bird-watching, going to the theater, and painting pictures. I am leaving soon to watch the wolves of Yellowstone National Park, a favorite pastime. I also like to drive to the Hudson River, get a hot dog from the vendor, and sit on the riverbank and eat it. I like lunch or dinner with my friends and visiting my kids.

◆ *Do you have any new books coming out soon?*

I have three books coming out soon: *Firestorm* and *Snowboard Twist*, both illustrated by Wendell Minor, and *Charlie's Ravens*. Three others are "in the works."

◆ *You've said that you have taken in many different pets from the wild. Do you still do this? What pets (even if not wild) do you have?*

I cannot have wild pets anymore. Today there are many rules governing the raising of wild things, and I do not have a permit to do this. However, I have an African gray parrot whose name is Tocca Two. (*Tocca* means sunshine in Swahili.) She says, "Who let the dogs out, who, who who who," "What the heck, let's go fishing," "Galápagos George," "Here comes that durn squirrel," and much, much more. I just told her I was busy writing and she said, "Who cares!"

Chapter Charter:
Questions to Guide Your Reading

The following questions will help you think about the important parts of each chapter.

Part I: Amaroq, the wolf

- What has happened to Miyax? How would you feel if you were in her situation?
- What is Alaska like? What words does the author use to tell us what it's like there?
- What has happened to Miyax's father? What does she tell the reader about him? How do you think Miyax feels about her father? How can you tell?
- Miyax has not eaten for three days. She had been certain the wolves would provide her with meat by now, but they have not. When she realizes she will still not have food for another day, she says to herself, "So I won't ... and that's that." Would you have been as practical and calm if you were this hungry and still couldn't eat?
- Which wolf does Miyax identify as the leader? What does she learn about him that lets her know he is the leader? Whom does she compare this wolf to?
- How do the wolves seem to be communicating with one another? How does Miyax attempt to communicate with them?
- Who is Daniel? How do you think Miyax feels about him?

- Where is Miyax going when she runs away from home? Why do you think she is leaving her home to go to this place?
- Miyax calls the wolf leader the "wealthy wolf." What does this mean to her as an Eskimo? What does the word *wealth* mean to you? Is your definition different from Miyax's definition?
- What does Miyax name each of the wolves? What are her reasons for picking these names? Do you think the names are good ones? Why or why not?
- What does Miyax look like? Do you think she likes the way she looks? Who does she want to look like?
- What happens to Miyax the first time she runs off from her frost heave without watching where she is going? What lesson does she learn from this?
- Miyax makes up a song about Amaroq. What do you think its words mean?
- Why does Miyax worry so much about the approach of winter on the tundra? In what ways does the author tell you that winter is coming?
- What was the pecking order, or order of importance, of the wolves at the beginning of the section? What is the order like at the end of the first section?

Part II: Miyax, the girl
- What has happened to Miyax's mother? What was her father's reaction to this?
- To Miyax, the years she spent at the seal camp with her father "were beautiful color spots in her memory." What different colors does Miyax associate with her different memories?
- Kapugen tells Miyax, "Wolves are brotherly. They love each other, and if you learn to speak to them, they will love you too."

Based on what you have read so far, do you think this is true? How so?

- What is Miyax's summer name? Why does she have a name different from the one the Eskimos use for her? Does she like this name?
- Overnight, Miyax's whole life changes when she is taken away from her father and the seal camp. Has something important in your family ever happened that fast? How did you react?
- The narrator tells the reader, "With that I became Julie." How is Miyax's life in Mekoryuk different from her life at the seal camp? Which one do you think is better? Which one does Miyax seem to think is better?
- What do you think it means when Miyax says, "Daylight is spelled A-M-Y"?
- Why does Miyax want to leave Mekoryuk? What allows her to leave and go to Barrow? Is she happy in Barrow?
- What does Miyax realize about Naka? How does this affect Miyax and Naka's family?
- What advice does Miyax remember after Daniel attacks her? What does she decide to do as a result?
- What does it mean when Miyax tells the reader, "Julie is gone. I am Miyax now." How does Miyax act when she uses that name? How does she act when she is being called Julie?

Part III: Kapugen, the hunter
- How is Jello acting toward Miyax? Why do you think he is acting this way? What does Miyax remember Kapugen saying about lone wolves?
- After Jello steals Miyax's pack with her supplies and food, how does she feel? How would you feel if this happened to you?

- How does Miyax feel about Amaroq? How do you know?
- What is Miyax's relationship like with Kapu? What things does the pup do that tell you this?
- How does Miyax feel when she sees the oil drum? Why do you think she feels this way?
- What does the oil drum mean for the fate of the wolves? What happens to Amaroq when he gets closer to the oil drums?
- Miyax says, "The pink room is red with your blood." Whom is she saying this to? What do you think she means?
- Who are Roland and Alice? Who are Atik and Uma? What does Miyax call them?
- How does Miyax find out that Kapugen might be alive?
- What does Miyax find that Kapugen's life is like when she goes into Kangik? What does she think about the way his life has turned out? How does she react when she sees the kind of life he is leading?
- What do you think Miyax is going to do in the end? Is it a good solution? What would you have done in her situation?

Plot: What's Happening?

"Julie pointed her boots toward Kapugen."

—*Julie of the Wolves*

Julie of the Wolves is the story of a young Eskimo girl named Julie (or Miyax, in Inuit, the language of the Eskimo people) who gets lost on the Alaskan tundra all alone. She is able to survive using the lessons her father taught her and with the help of a pack of wolves.

The story opens in the middle of Miyax's adventure. Thirteen-year-old Miyax is closely watching a pack of Arctic wolves. Miyax is lost on the tundra on the northern slope of Alaska. Her father, Kapugen, taught her many lessons about survival. She knows that when he was lost once, he looked to the Arctic wolves for food and they provided it for him, allowing him to survive.

Miyax is studying a pack of wolves near the frost heave where she has set up a camp for herself. She is trying to figure out if they have a way of communicating with one another. She believes that if she can learn their language, she can ask them for food.

There is one very large, black wolf that Miyax names Amaroq.
This wolf reminds her of her father because he walks with his
head up high and the other wolves look to Amaroq for guidance.

In addition to Amaroq, the the wolf pack consists of a mother wolf,
whom Miyax names Silver. There are two other adult wolves that
she names Nails and Jello, and five wolf puppies, too. Miyax sees
something special in the black pup and she names him Kapu.

The wolves begin to accept Miyax into their pack. When she is
able, Miyax shares the meat hunted by the wolves.

Miyax realizes that once it is winter on the tundra, the wolves
will leave to roam around looking for food. This scares her
because she has come to depend on the wolves. She remembers
something that Kapugen told her: "Change your ways when fear
seizes, for it usually means you are doing something wrong."
Miyax promises herself that she will change the way she depends
on the wolves. She hunts for food on her own and is successful!

Winter arrives and the wolves leave their dens to wander the
tundra. Miyax has flashbacks, or memories, about her life before
she was lost on the tundra. She remembers the day her mother
died. On this day, Kapugen zipped her up inside his parka with
him and walked all the way to the seal camp, where the two lived
for a while.

Miyax remembers loving her time with Kapugen at the seal camp.
She has beautiful, colorful memories of the traditional Eskimos

there. The Eskimos there are at one with nature and their environment. Kapugen teaches her many things about how to survive off the land and the animals. He tells her, "Yes, you are Eskimo. And never forget it. We live as no other people can, for we truly understand the earth." They live very differently from the Eskimos in a town called Mekoryuk. In Mekoryuk the Americanized Eskimos called her and Kapugen by their English names, Julie and Charlie.

Miyax recalls the day her aunt, Martha, who lives in Mekoryuk, comes with orders to take Miyax away from Kapugen. Miyax does not want to leave her father. Before she is forced to leave with her aunt, Kapugen tells Miyax that if she is not happy in Mekoryuk, he will arrange it so that she can marry his friend's son, Daniel, when she turns thirteen. She will be able to go back to living like a traditional Eskimo. She never sees Kapugen again and suddenly finds herself living in an Americanized town where people call her Julie.

Miyax, now Julie, tries to accept her new life. It is hard for her because the urban Eskimos make fun of her for not knowing about their modern ways of living. One day a mainland American man drives up to her and hands her a letter from his daughter in San Francisco, California. His daughter, Amy, is looking for a pen pal in Alaska, and Miyax will be it! In her letter, Amy describes the mainland United States and invites her pen pal to come and visit her. Miyax sees the United States as a way out of Mekoryuk. She says, "Daylight is spelled A-M-Y."

Julie also wants to get away from Aunt Martha, who lives among the urbanized Eskimos. Martha does not like Miyax's hair, friends, and hobbies because they are becoming less and less traditional. One day a man arrives with a signed agreement between Kapugen and Kapugen's friend, Naka. It is the agreement that Kapugen told Miyax he would make when she was taken away from him. It says that Miyax can go and live with Naka and his wife if she marries their son, Daniel.

Miyax agrees to go to Barrow to marry Daniel. When she arrives, she is disappointed to find that Daniel is mildly mentally retarded. She is relieved when Nusan, Naka's wife, tells her that Daniel will be like a brother to her. But the next day, Miyax is surprised to find that she and Daniel are being married in an official ceremony.

Miyax becomes friends with a girl named Pearl, who introduces Miyax to other kids in town. Pearl tells Miyax not to worry about her marriage to Daniel—that it is just a formality that no one takes too seriously. Miyax settles into her life in Barrow. She continues receiving letters from Amy and dreams of living in San Francisco.

One night, Daniel comes home, where Miyax is alone. Daniel says that the other boys tease him about Miyax, and so he attacks her. Miyax is scared and upset and remembers Kapugen's wise words again: "When fear seizes, change what you are doing. You are doing something wrong."

She immediately packs up some of her belongings. She leaves Naka and Nusan's house and heads for San Francisco, declaring to herself that she is no longer Julie. Her name is Miyax.

Miyax's flashback is over and the reader is back on the tundra with her. The wolves are gone. She returns to her camp to find it has been destroyed and her food has been stolen. Jello appears and she realizes he is responsible for the damage. She has little food left, but remains hopeful. She packs up and leaves the site, heading toward Point Hope.

One night while she is asleep, Jello suddenly appears and steals her pack with all of her belongings in it! Miyax is scared and is almost ready to give up hope.

While in search of her pack, Miyax comes across Jello's dead body. Amaroq has killed Jello for acting out against Miyax. As she continues toward Point Hope, Miyax becomes close with the black wolf pup, Kapu. Kapu looks after her, just as Amaroq has done.

Miyax now loves and appreciates her surroundings. She sees how she and the wolves fit into nature. The author tells us, "Out here she understood how she fitted into the scheme of the moon and stars and the constant rise and fall of life on the earth."

Miyax finds a small young plover bird that is lost. She takes him in and names him Tornait. As she is walking she hears a plane overhead. She knows that in the plane are gussak hunters, looking for wolves. Although she tries to protect them, Amaroq is shot and killed by the hunters, and Kapu is badly injured.

Miyax mourns the loss of Amaroq and knows that although he is gone, his spirit is with her. She decides that the American way of life isn't all good and prefers the life she's been living on her own—the life of a traditional Eskimo.

Miyax is getting closer and closer to Point Hope, but she no longer cares about reaching the settlement. She is happy spending her days with Kapu and Tornait, living off the land. One day a family comes upon Miyax's camp. Atik and Uma tell Miyax of the town they live in, called Kangik. They tell Miyax about Atik's mentor, the greatest of all Eskimo hunters, Kapugen. Miyax is shocked and confused. Could this be her father Kapugen? She decides to find out.

When Miyax gets to Kangik, she finds that the Kapugen living there is, in fact, her father. He explains that he tried to go back to Mekoryuk to find Miyax, but she was not there. Kapugen has married a gussak woman named Ellen and flies an airplane. Miyax leaves Kapugen's house and is confused about the changes in her father's life and how it differs from her experiences living alone on the tundra.

Miyax heads back out onto the tundra and Tornait suddenly dies. She buries him, then sings herself a song about Amaroq. Then she points her boots back toward Kapugen's house.

Thinking about the plot

- Why has Miyax (Julie) run away from home?
- How is it that she is lost on the tundra?
- How does Miyax (Julie) feel about American ways of life? How does she feel about traditional Eskimo ways of life? Do her feelings about these remain constant throughout the novel?
- What has Kapugen taught Miyax?

"...the tundra was an ocean of grass on which she was circling around and around."

—*Julie of the Wolves*

The setting of a book is where and when the story takes place. *Julie of the Wolves* takes place entirely in Alaska in the twentieth century. Jean Craighead George actually traveled to Alaska, studying the place, its animals, and its people, before writing *Julie of the Wolves*. Her thorough research enabled her to create a very realistic, detailed world for Miyax's adventure.

Place

The author places her heroine on the northern slope of the Alaskan tundra. Although Alaska is part of the United States, it is not part of the continental United States. Like Hawaii, Alaska is not attached to the mainland United States. It is attached to Canada and juts out into the Pacific Ocean near the Arctic Circle.

Miyax is lost on the tundra. The tundra is bare and flat and covered in short grasses, making it greenish brown in the summer. Because the Alaskan tundra is so far north, it's usually very cold. It only reaches about 40 degrees Fahrenheit there in the summer. During the summer there are days when the sun never sets on the tundra. In fact, in Barrow, Alaska, the sun is always up between mid-May and early August. There are eighty-four days when it's never dark outside. This is because at this time of year, the Arctic Circle, the northernmost part of the earth, is tilted toward the sun. If you look at a globe you'll see that it's tilted to represent this angle. Miyax describes this time of year: "The sun slid down the sky, hung still for a moment, then started up again. It was midnight." In the summer the ground thaws a little bit. A thin layer of soil defrosts just enough for very short grasses to grow. Strong winds blow year-round, preventing taller plants or trees from growing. Miyax looks out on "a vast lawn of grass and moss."

In the winter, it's usually snowy there. Miyax observes its beauty when she says, "Her icy sled jingled over the wind-swept lakes. . . . the stars grew brighter as the hours passed and the tundra began to glow, for the snow reflected each twinkle a billion times over, turning the night to silver." At this time of year, the northernmost part of the earth is pointed away from the sun, so it is dark all day long for a very long time. For sixty-six days in the heart of the winter, the sun never rises above the horizon. The author describes this time of the year: ". . . the land would be white with snow and in three months the long Arctic night that lasted sixty-six days would darken the top of the world." With little or no sun, extremely cold temperatures (as low as 25 degrees below zero), and the fierce winds, there is very little life on the tundra in the winter. The author says, "Snowstorms came and went; the wind blew constantly."

The ground is frozen, so little plant life can grow. Without plants, small animals do not have much food to live on, and without small animals to eat, larger animals are also scarce. There are a few animals that have gradually adapted to the harsh Arctic environment. Mammals such as Arctic foxes, wolves, and hares live there. Arctic birds include the snowy owl and the ptarmigan. Some of the animals that live there, like the hare and fox, turn white when winter comes. They have adapted over many years to blend in with the snowy environment so that they will be hidden from their predators. The author explains: "The fox's brown fur of summer was splotched with white patches. . . . he would soon be white like snow." Some of the birds that inhabit the tundra, like the terns, only live there in the summer. When winter approaches, they migrate south to warmer temperatures. The caribou that sometimes Miyax lived on also migrate south in the fall to escape the harsh winter temperatures and to find more plentiful sources of food.

In the Arctic, a phenomenon known as aurora borealis, or the northern lights, occurs. The aurora borealis is glimmering ribbons of colored light that flash across the sky. This happens because there are electrically charged particles from the sun in the air. The particles are drawn to Earth's atmosphere by the magnetic field of the North Pole. These particles bump into Earth's atmosphere and release energy that people see as bands of light. The best place to watch this amazing sight is from Barrow, Alaska, between August and April. Miyax describes this beautiful natural phenomenon: "Fountains of green fire rose from the earth and shot to the top of the black velvet sky. Red and white lights sprayed out of the green."

In the second section of *Julie of the Wolves*, the author changes the story's location. The reader is suddenly in the populated areas of Alaska. Miyax spends time in both the village of Mekoryuk and the larger city of Barrow. Alaskan villages are small, with only a couple of hundred inhabitants. Villagers tend to live in low-roofed houses. Towns have only a few large buildings. Most manufactured goods are brought in by boat or airplane because the harsh weather makes driving difficult. Food is obtained by hunting Arctic animals. The people must wear heavy parkas and boots to stay warm.

These town settings are brought to life by the people who live in them. Eskimos are the native people who live in the Arctic and sub-Arctic regions of North America and Siberia. The word *Eskimo* is not actually an Eskimo word. Translated, it means "eaters of raw meat" and is a term that was given to the native people by the Algonquin Indians of northern Canada. The Algonquins called their neighbors this because they wore animal-skin clothing and were very good hunters. The name became commonly used by European explorers who encountered them and it has stuck. The term used by the people themselves is *Inuit*, which means "real people."

Some Eskimo, or Inuit, people settle on rivers and survive by fishing. Others settle inland and follow the caribou herds. Most settle on the coasts and survive by hunting maritime animals like seals, walrus, and whales. When Miyax was a small girl, she spent time with her father at a seal camp. She describes it: "There was Kapugen's little house of driftwood, not far from the beach. It was rosy-gray on the outside. Inside, it was gold-brown.

Walrus tusks gleamed and drums, harpoons, and man's knives decorated the walls. The sealskin kayak beside the door glowed. . . . The ocean was green and white. . . ." Miyax remembered the seals there, too: "She saw the soft eyes of the seals on the ice. . . . Then the ice would turn red."

The ability of the Eskimo people to adapt successfully to the Arctic environment is due to their inventive culture. They are skilled in taking natural resources and making them into useful devices. For example, their traditional clothing is made from animal skins. Miyax makes snowshoes for herself using frozen strips of meat, and an igloo home with blocks of frozen snow and ice.

Time

Although Jean Craighead George does not specify exactly when her story takes place, the reader can assume it is the late twentieth century. The majority of the story takes place in the wild, vast tundra, where things seem to never change. There is little there to indicate the time period, except the oil barrels Miyax sees on the tundra. They are a sure sign of modern America, where the oil industry is so important.

The Eskimo, or Inuit, people are far away from the mainland United States, but they have most of the modern conveniences mainland residents have today. There are cars, like the one Amy's dad drives. There are gas stoves, like the one in Aunt Martha's house. Airplanes take people from place to place, like the one Miyax travels in to Barrow, and the one used by the hunters who kill Amaroq. When Miyax meets Pearl, the two spend time at the Quonset. The people there are drinking Coca-Cola, listening to rock music, and wearing blue jeans.

All of these things probably remind you of things you see every day, so the story can't take place too far in the past or too far in the future.

Thinking about the setting

- What are the different seasons on the Alaskan tundra like?
- What does the author tell us about the people and animals of Alaska?
- What are some clues from the author that tell the reader when the story takes place?

"...my heart belonged to the wilderness."

—Jean Craighead George

The theme of a book is the subject matter about which the author is writing. Themes are the main ideas on which the book is based. *Julie of the Wolves* has several themes such as survival in difficult circumstances, pride in one's culture, and courage.

Cultural pride

Cultural pride is a very important theme in *Julie of the Wolves*. The Eskimo, or Inuit (as they call themselves), people have lived in harmony with their environment for thousands of years. On her trip to Barrow, Alaska, to research *Julie of the Wolves*, Jean Craighead George witnessed one of the ways in which the people live by old traditions. While she was there, an Inuit boy led her onto the ocean ice to show her a group of Inuit men who were carving up a huge bowhead whale that they had just caught. George was deeply moved by what she saw. She says, "Later I would learn that I had been observing a two-thousand-year-old ritual of carving the whale for distribution among Eskimo people."

Kapugen tells Miyax: "The Eskimos live as no other people can, for we truly understand the earth." It is his words that she remembers throughout her adventures. Kapugen has taught her that the traditional ways of the Eskimo people are all she really needs to live a full and happy life.

Just as Miyax was taught, she keeps her clothing dry by placing it in whale bladder. She sings old ritual feast songs when she catches owls to eat. When the wolves provide her with a caribou killing, she pays tribute by raising her arms to the sun. She also pays tribute to the sun itself, when it finally rises on January 24. She appreciates how hard her people work to make use of caribou killings when nature provides them with one. And she cherishes the caribou's liver as she eats it, understanding that it's Eskimo tradition for women to eat the liver because it has the most nutrients.

Miyax remembers with great fondness the lessons she learned from her father at the seal camp. The author says, "He told her that the birds and animals all had languages, and if you listened and watched them you could learn about their enemies, where their food lay and when big storms were coming."

At different times during the story, however, the reader sees that Miyax also feels that more modern, Americanized ways of life might be better. When she thinks of the mainland United States she thinks of what Amy had told her about it: "Julie learned about television, sports cars, blue jeans, bikinis, hero sandwiches, and wall-to-wall carpeting in the high school Amy would soon be attending."

When she lives in Mekoryuk, Miyax is teased by the Eskimo girls there for not knowing more about American mainland culture. She has not gone to school like they have, and she doesn't know about modern conveniences, like gas cooking stoves. When she catches a glimpse of her reflection while lost, she's happy that her face looks narrower than it does round. She looks more like a gussak, or white, girl than an Eskimo girl. However, when a hunter in an airplane kills Amaroq, Miyax begins to think of mainland America as bad. She sees it as a culture that kills beautiful animals for money.

Even though she feels the push and pull of two different cultures, Miyax is more influenced by her traditional upbringing than anything else. It is this upbringing that finally makes her feel content in her life wandering the tundra. Miyax learns to live on her own and is at peace with the weather and the animals. After Amaroq's death, the author tells us, "When she thought of San Francisco, she thought about the airplane and the fire and blood and the flashes and death. When she took out her needle and sewed, she thought about peace and Amaroq."

This conflict between the traditional Eskimo way of life and modern American life haunts Miyax the most when she finds out Kapugen is still alive. The author tells us: "Eskimos turn to their elders for leadership and wisdom and they respect the animals and know that they couldn't live without them." Although Kapugen could now be a part of her life again, Miyax does not know how to feel about him. He is living a less traditional life than what she remembered. He seems to be swayed by modern ways now, and she is determined not to let those ways be a part of her life. Should she swallow her pride and stay with Kapugen anyway? Or should she live in the way she has come to enjoy and leave him again?

George has shown the reader both the old and new Inuit ways of life and explores the tension between them. In the end, she leaves this question open-ended. The reader does not know for certain which Miyax will decide is better.

Survival

Another important theme in *Julie of the Wolves* is survival. Miyax finds herself in a very challenging situation and has to be completely self-reliant, or dependent on herself, to make it through. Miyax looks to the wolves and to what she has learned from her culture to keep herself alive in the harsh conditions on the tundra.

Miyax begins trying to communicate with the wolves. She feels, based on what her father has told her, that if she can make them understand that she needs their help, they will provide it. She does this by closely observing their behaviors and mimicking what they do until she convinces the wolves that she is one of them. It works and the wolves accept her into their pack. They give her portions of the food they have, and they protect her from harm, such as when a grizzly bear gets too close to her camp.

The wolves also provide Miyax with companionship while she is lost. With no other people around, Miyax could have been very lonely. Having companions is another important part of surviving. She forms very close, special friendships with certain wolves in the pack. She was especially bonded to Amaroq, and later on, to Kapu. They make her feel loved and comfortable when her family and friends are not there to do that for her. Later, she befriends Tornait, the small bird she finds that is also lost. In some ways, Tornait is a kindred spirit to Miyax. He is small and all by himself, just like Miyax. Having a companion, even a small bird, helps Miyax feel less alone on the tundra and helps give her the courage to continue her journey.

To feel even more comfortable, Miyax does things that make her happy. She decorates her camps, carves a totem, dances, and sings songs to celebrate nature.

Even without the help of the wolves, Miyax may have survived. Inuit traditions emphasized making do with what nature provides. Inuit people can live by using resources from their natural environment rather than relying only on modern technology. Miyax's father has taught her many skills that allow her to do what her ancestors traditionally did to survive. She could have easily become discouraged and given up when she found herself lost. She could have done this even more easily at certain times, like when Jello stole her food and the pack with all her supplies.

Instead of giving up, she uses the lessons of her people to help her. Miyax makes snowshoes out of frozen caribou meat to travel on, she sews a new mitten for herself out of animal skins and rabbit fur, and she even builds herself an igloo home. These are things that adults probably would have done for Miyax. But when she is lost, there are no adults to help her. A reviewer said, "It is not so much the wolves who save her as her own native wit, her inborn sense of how to use, not fight, the elements." She is able to survive on her own because she has learned to be resourceful.

Courage

A third important theme in *Julie of the Wolves* is courage. Kapugen had taught Miyax that "fear can sometimes cripple a person to the point that he cannot think or act." Kapugen has also told Miyax, "When fear seizes, change what you are doing. You are doing something wrong."

Miyax shows her courage many times. It is brave of Miyax to leave her aunt. She was not happy with her life, so she decided to go live with Daniel's family, whom she didn't know at all. This took great courage. It is also very brave of her to leave Daniel. Something bad happened to her, and like her father taught her, she changed what she was doing. She picks herself up and leaves the life that included what frightened her: Daniel. Miyax also decides that she will travel to another part of the world all by herself. She will walk to the ship at Point Hope and make a new start for herself in San Francisco. This takes a lot of courage to do as well. Not many thirteen-year-old kids would act with such bravery, especially without having an adult around to support them.

Miyax's courage is seen the most when she is around the wolf pack. She bravely tries to begin communicating with these large, sometimes ferocious, wild animals. Even when they growl or snap at her with their teeth, she lets herself be afraid for only a moment. She moves past her fear and keeps trying to understand them, and to make them understand her.

It takes a lot of bravery for Miyax to persist in the harsh conditions of the tundra. Even when she thinks all is lost, she will not let herself become so afraid that she cannot help herself. She heeds Kapugen's words well.

Thinking about themes
• What do you think is the most important theme in *Julie of the Wolves*?
• Do you think that the traditional Eskimo ways are better than the more modern Eskimo ways? Why or why not?
• When have you had to be courageous?

Characters: Who Are These People, Anyway?

The way an author develops the people in a story is called characterization. The writer helps the reader understand the people in the book by describing what they look like, how they act, the things they say and do, how they interact with the other characters, and how they react to different situations. This is a list of the characters in *Julie of the Wolves*, followed by descriptions of the most important ones.

People

Miyax (Julie)	main character, thirteen years old when the novel begins
Kapugen	Miyax's father
Martha	Miyax's aunt
Daniel	Miyax's husband
Naka	Daniel's father; good friend of Kapugen
Nusan	Daniel's mother
Pearl	Miyax's friend

Animals

Amaroq	the leader of the wolf pack
Kapu	the leader of the wolf pups
Silver	the female in the wolf pack
Nails	male adult wolf
Jello	male adult wolf

Sister	the smallest wolf pup
Zing, Zat, Zit	the three other wolf pups
Tornait	the small, lost bird that Miyax befriends

Miyax (Julie): Miyax is the heroine, or main female character, of *Julie of the Wolves*. Her Eskimo name is Miyax. Her English name is Julie. When the novel starts, Miyax is thirteen years old. Miyax is a brave, patient, and resourceful girl. Miyax's mother has died. She has a close relationship with her father, Kapugen, but he has disappeared. Miyax believes in the traditional ways of the Eskimo people. She loves and respects animals and nature. She also sometimes wants to be more like the gussak, or white people, of the mainland United States.

When Miyax gets lost on the tundra running away from Daniel, the reader sees how she is resourceful and brave. Miyax uses all the elements of nature and the teachings of the Eskimo people to survive on her own when she gets lost. She creates shelters for herself, she finds ways of getting food to eat, and she eventually figures out which direction she needs to be going to get to the coast.

Although Miyax gets scared sometimes when she is lost, she keeps a level head. She remembers the teachings of her father and does not let her fear get the best of her. She uses what Kapugen has taught her to communicate with the wolves she encounters on the tundra. She also remembers the cultural pride Kapugen has instilled in her. Miyax thanks the animals for keeping her alive: "Impulsively, she paid tribute to the spirit of the caribou by lifting her arms to the sun." She realizes that she would not be able to live without them.

Although Miyax feels great pride about her Eskimo heritage, she sometimes feels confused about whether or not it is really the best way to live. She is exposed to modern ways of living during her time in Barrow and is drawn to cities, like San Francisco, on the mainland. In Mekoryuk, Miyax wants to fit in better with the girls her age by going to school and having jewelry. She wants to wear her hair short like white women, and wishes her face looked more like a gussak girl's. Miyax is curious to see television and high school. But these feelings are usually outweighed by more positive feelings about traditional Eskimo ways of life.

Miyax develops a very close, unusual bond with the wolves. The reader sees how deeply she can care for animals. She loves them because they provide her with food. But Miyax also loves them because they protect her from harm on the tundra and because they act as companions when there are no other people around. She looks to them for comfort and company. Miyax tries to protect the wolves from the harmful hunters, so the reader sees how much she loves them in this way, too. She mourns Amaroq's death a great deal. She even creates a totem of him so that his spirit can always be with her.

Miyax is a patient girl. Just as Kapugen said, good things happen to those who are patient. When she is learning to communicate with the wolves, it takes quite a long time for them to accept her into their pack. She does things wrong, and they push her away. But she persists and waits for them to feel comfortable with her presence. Miyax's patience is also shown when she is able to capture birds to eat without any help. She searches and waits by nests until she finally finds food for herself. The food tastes that much better because Miyax had to wait patiently for it to come to her.

Kapugen: Kapugen is Miyax's father. He is a believer in the traditional ways of the Eskimo, or Inuit, people. Kapugen's wife, Miyax's mother, has died. When Miyax was younger, Kapugen disappeared. People said that he had paddled his kayak into the Bering Sea to go seal hunting and never came back. Although Kapugen is not physically present for most of the story, his personality is brought to life through Miyax's memories of him.

Miyax remembers that the day her mother died, Kapugen put Miyax inside his parka and took her to the seal camp with him. There, he taught his daughter all the traditional Eskimo ways of life. He taught her to be brave, he taught her to be resourceful, he taught her to respect plants and animals and all of nature. Kapugen taught Miyax how to communicate with animals and that she could survive off of the land if she wanted to. When Miyax is taken away from Kapugen, he is sad, but he lets her go. He thinks this is best for her and wants her to go to school. The reader sees that Kapugen loves Miyax very much because of all the things he has taken the time to teach her and because he only wants what he thinks is best for her.

Kapugen is known as one of the most wise and skilled living Eskimo hunters. He is well-respected by other Eskimos. Even though Miyax has always thought this, her beliefs about her father are confirmed when she meets Atik and Uma. They speak very highly of Kapugen and say that he is the greatest of all living Eskimo hunters. The couple say that he is a wealthy man because he possesses intelligence, fearlessness, and love. He is the leader of their town, Kangik.

When Miyax sees her father again for the first time in a long time, the reader learns that he is living a more modern way of life. He flies an airplane and uses it to hunt. He lives in a modern house, with electric lamps and an electric stove. He has married a gussak woman. This makes the reader question what Kapugen's true beliefs are. The author cuts off the story before this question can be answered, leaving it up to the reader to decide.

Amaroq: Amaroq is the leader of the wolf pack that Miyax communicates with on the tundra. Amaroq is large, dominant, and protective. His senses are keen and accurate. Amaroq reminds Miyax of Kapugen.

When Miyax first meets Amaroq, she sees that he is large and black. He stands above the other wolves and holds out his chest. The pack looks to him for guidance, so the reader knows that Amaroq is wise. The other wolves in his pack pay tribute to Amaroq by smothering him with affectionate gestures to show that they appreciate his leadership.

Amaroq takes good care of his pack by providing them with as much food as he can. He hunts caribou and even lets Miyax have some. He allows Miyax to become a member of his pack, and so he takes care of her just as he does the rest. The author shows how Amaroq takes care of Miyax when he protects her from the dangerous grizzly bear. Amaroq also removes Jello from his pack by killing him because Jello was a threat to Miyax.

Amaroq's senses are very sharp. For much of the book, Miyax must be on her hands and knees for the wolves to accept her. Even in a thick fog, through which Amaroq cannot see, he knows when Miyax is standing on two legs, proving that this good leader can sense things he cannot see. Eventually, Amaroq accepts Miyax for what she is and allows her to approach him while she stands upright.

Thinking about the characters

- Which of the characters do you like the most? the least? Why?
- Is Miyax similar to kids you know who are the same age? How are they different?
- Is there a character in *Julie of the Wolves* who you think is a little like you? How so?
- Do you think any of the characters are like the others? What similarities do you see?

It's a winner!

In addition to winning the 1973 John Newbery Medal, *Julie of the Wolves* was also a National Book Award finalist and has been recognized as one of the 10 best American children's books in 200 years by the Children's Literature Association. These are some very important honors.

Before *Julie of the Wolves* was an award-winning book, it received much praise from literary reviewers. A reviewer from *School Library Journal* said, "George has captured the subtle nuances of Eskimo life, animal habits, the pain of growing up, and combines these elements into a thrilling adventure which is, at the same time, a poignant love story." What this reviewer means is that the author shows the many different aspects of the ways Eskimos live, the ways animals live, and how hard it is to be an adolescent. The author combines these three things and creates a great adventure story. The reader gets to know Miyax, a young girl trying to find her place in the world. She is battling to survive in the tundra while trying to figure out who she is. At the same time, Jean Craighead George has written a love story. The reader sees how much Kapugen loves Miyax and vice versa. The reader also sees how much Miyax and the wolves love one another and how much Miyax loves her native culture.

According to *Booklist* magazine, "the well-written, empathetic story effectively evokes the nature of wolves and the traditional Eskimo way of life giving way before the relentless onslaught of civilization." The reviewer from this publication feels that Jean Craighead George has shown what Eskimo life was like before it began to be modernized, and how the American, modern way started creeping into the Eskimo culture and wouldn't go away. More and more modern methods and objects keep replacing traditional ways of life in this culture.

Horn Book magazine called *Julie of the Wolves* "a book of timeless, perhaps even classic dimensions." By using the words *timeless* and *classic*, this reviewer thinks the book will speak to its readers as much in future years as it did when it was first written.

Age disagreement

Most of the reviews that *Julie of the Wolves* received are positive. But there were some people who thought the book was not appropriate for kids in some ways. A school district in Littleton, Colorado, tried to move the book from its sixth-grade reading list to its high school reading list because it contains references to family alcoholism, abuse, and divorce. What they were specifically referring to was Naka's alcoholism, the way he hit his wife when he was drinking, and the fact that Miyax wanted to divorce her husband, Daniel. This dispute was settled, and the book was left on the school's sixth-grade reading list because the author shows how the characters overcome problems and show good decision-making skills.

Thinking about what others think about
Julie of the Wolves

- Should Jean Craighead George's book have won lots of awards? Are there other award-winning books you have read that were better or worse? How so?
- Are the messages and themes and lessons taught in *Julie of the Wolves* important now? Do you think they will be more or less important in the future? How so?
- Is it okay that the author included some sensitive issues and events in *Julie of the Wolves*? Do you think anything should have been left out?

Glossary

Here are some words that are used in *Julie of the Wolves*. Knowing what these words mean will help you better understand the novel.

amber a yellowish brown color

ambrosia something extremely pleasing to taste or smell

bounty a reward offered for the capture of an animal

bravado conduct that is foolish and adventurous

caribou a large North American mammal of the deer family. Caribou are related to reindeer.

carrion dead and rotting flesh

concave curved inward, like the inside surface of a dish

contort to twist something out of its usual shape

croon to sing or speak in a gentle, nurturing way

deference respect or esteem shown to an older or more superior person or creature

deft skillful, quick, and neat

derisively in a ridiculing or scornful manner

deviate to do something differently from the usual way

discern to distinguish between; to recognize as different

dispel to put an end to something

elated very pleased and excited

enamored to be in love with

evoke to bring to mind; to call forth

flail to wave or thrash something

forage to go in search of food

grovel to be unnaturally humble and polite to someone because you are afraid of the person or because you think he or she is very important

gussak the Inuit word for a person who looks more Caucasian than Eskimo

harpoon a long spear with an attached rope that can be thrown or shot out of a special gun. It is usually used for hunting large fish or whales.

hoist to lift something heavy

improvise to do the best you can with what is available

incorrigible not manageable

instill to put into a person's mind slowly, over a period of time

knoll a small hill

lair a place where a wild animal rests and sleeps

larder a small room or pantry in which food is stored

monotony without change; going on and on in a boring way

morsel a small piece of food

nomadic wandering around instead of living in one place

pinnacle a peak; the highest point

plaintive sad and mournful

plumage a bird's feathers

predator an animal that lives by hunting other animals for food

predicament an awkward or difficult situation

preen when a bird cleans and arranges its feathers

quell to stop or crush by force

quiver to tremble or vibrate

refrain to stop yourself from doing something

remote far away, isolated, or distant

saunter to walk in a slow, leisurely, or casual way

shaman a person who uses magic to control events or cure the sick

sheath a holder for a knife, sword, or dagger

stifle to hold back or stop

strewn covering a surface with things that have been scattered or sprinkled

sustain to keep something going

taut stretched tight

ulo an Eskimo woman's knife

undulate to rise and fall

vitality energy and liveliness

wane to get smaller in size

wean to start giving a baby food other than its mother's milk

writhe to twist and turn around, as in pain

"I kept on writing and illustrating, for this is what I did well because I loved it."

—Jean Craighead George

Jean Craighead George loves to write. She has been doing it since she was a little girl. From the time she was in the third grade she knew that she wanted to be a writer. Each day, beginning right after breakfast until three o'clock in the afternoon, Jean writes. She has always loved words, and writing gives her a way to share her knowledge and ideas with children and adults.

Jean Craighead George's main motivation for writing is to share with readers her love of nature. She says, "All I wish to do is tell the story of our North American animals and plants, hoping my readers will come to love them as I do in all their magnificence." When people read her books, they gain an appreciation of the animals she writes about. Her books can turn people who don't know much about animals into animal lovers. For people who already adore animals, her writing can make those feelings even stronger.

Another reason Jean Craighead George enjoys writing is because she wants to teach young people new things. Some readers are just beginning to learn about the natural world, and she makes it come to life. By reading her books, young people learn without even realizing it. She says, "I really believe in stories to bring children into knowledge. You can hang so much information on a good story, and they aren't even aware they're getting it, but pretty soon they know the whole ecology of the tundra and the life history of the wolf and they want more and they go to other books." Jean finds that once her readers get a small sample of how interesting the natural world can be by reading her books, they just want to know more and more.

Jean Craighead George's books are dramatic partly because her writing is so beautiful. But they are also compelling because she includes many true-to-life details. She thinks it's very important to give her readers an accurate picture of the worlds she creates in her books. She says, "We [adults] owe children reliable knowledge. The very best we can give them." To do this, George researches her books very thoroughly. She spends time reading about and visiting the places in her stories so that she can give exact information about them. Before she wrote *Julie of the Wolves,* Jean visited Barrow, Alaska, and studied wolves, the land and climate of the tundra, as well as the traditions and teachings of native Inuit people. She did this to make sure that her book was as real and true as possible.

To come up with her characters, Jean Craighead George often makes them a bit like herself or people she knows well, like her brothers. For example, Miyax's character is a little like Jean herself. Jean says, "Most writers put a bit of themselves into their characters." Then she takes the character she has created and thinks of a problem that the character needs to solve. George says that she finds ideas for her stories in everything she encounters. "I'm asleep if I can't get any ideas for writing. Ideas are everywhere. Your shoes must have been many places with tales to tell. The rain coming down the windowpane is a tale to tell—and on and on," she says.

When Jean won the John Newbery Medal for *Julie of the Wolves*, it meant so much to her because it was a sign that she had touched children's lives. She had made something that affected children in a positive way. She says, ". . . the Newbery medal meant more to me than the Nobel or the Pulitzer Prize because it reached into childhood, into those years where books and characters last a lifetime."

- **And then?:** *Julie of the Wolves* ends with the sentence, "Julie pointed her boots toward Kapugen." The reader isn't sure what Miyax's future holds now that she has discovered that Kapugen is alive. Pick up where Jean Craighead George leaves off and write the next scene in the story. Will Miyax go back to her father? Will she decide to head back out into the wild by herself? You decide!

- **Pen it!:** In *Julie of the Wolves*, Miyax and Amy are pen pals. A pen pal is a buddy with whom you write back and forth, telling him or her about your life, where you live, your family, whatever is happening to you that you want to share. Find a pen pal for yourself! You can do this over e-mail, or the "snail mail" way by sending a letter through the post office. Make sure you check with an adult before corresponding over the Internet. Check out Kids' Space Connection at www.ks-connection.org for international pen pals.

- **Colors paint a picture:** When Miyax is at the seal camp with Kapugen, her memories are formed with colors. She associates each thing she encounters there with its colors. These colors create beautiful memories in her mind. Think about things that happened in you past. What colors do you remember seeing as they were happening? Do you remember the sand and ocean from a trip to the beach? Do you remember the snow and sleds from a snow day? Do you remember the uniforms from a sports outing? Whatever colors you remember, write about a memory by describing it with colors.

• **Animal tales:** *Julie of the Wolves* is the story of a girl interacting with wolves. She becomes as close to the wolves as many people become to each other. Is there an animal you care about a great deal? Write about your relationship with an animal or animals. This could be a pet, or a wild animal, or even an animal in a zoo. Even if the animal is no longer alive, what did it mean to you? What experiences did you have with this animal? What did it teach you?

• **Seasons of change:** As Miyax's story progresses, the seasons of the tundra progress, too. She gets lost in the summer, while the grasses still grow. But by the time she finds Kapugen, winter has come. What are the seasons like where you live? Write about them in a journal as they change over the course of the year.

- **Sing!:** Miyax makes up a song about Amaroq that she sings to praise him. Create a song of your own about something that interests you. Make up lyrics and a melody for it. Your song can be funny or silly, happy or sad. Sing about an animal, as Miyax does, or about things like school, or nature, or your family.

- **Locate it:** Where in the world is Alaska? Locate Alaska on a map of the United States. Where is the land that is tundra? Where are the cities and villages that Miyax lives in during the course of the book? Do you see Barrow? What about Mekoryuk? Make a map of Alaska for yourself. Be sure to clearly mark all the important places from the book.

- **Be a researcher:** Jean Craighead George did lots of thorough research before she wrote *Julie of the Wolves*. Go to your local library or jump onto the Internet to find out more about a portion of the book. Look up Arctic wolves or seals. Find out more about the tundra or Eskimo culture. You could even try to see some of these things in person. Even if you can't take a trip to Alaska, you can head to your local zoo to observe the animals there!

- **Cover to cover:** The cover of *Julie of the Wolves* shows Miyax (Julie) and Amaroq. The front cover of a book is important because it is what makes a first impression on the reader. It should reflect something meaningful or important about the book. If you were given the job of designing the book's cover, what picture would you use? Draw a new cover for *Julie of the Wolves* using images from the book that mean the most to you.

- **Speak the language:** Miyax is an Eskimo, or Inuit. The reader learns that her Inuit name is Miyax and her English name is Julie. Look up your own name to see what the closest Inuit word is for it. Then, look up the names of your family and friends. Find out what the Inuit word is for your favorite food or animal. Learn to say hello and good-bye. Then, teach your friends to say things in Inuit. It can be your secret code! Check out the University of Oregon's Yamada Language Center on Inuit/Inuktitut for lots of links to Inuit language resources: http://babel.uoregon.edu/yamada/guides/inuit.html.

- **Keep reading!:** After writing *Julie of the Wolves*, Jean Craighead George wrote two more books about Miyax. Are you curious about what is going to happen to Miyax when *Julie of the Wolves* ends? Find out! Go to your local library or bookstore and check out *Julie*, the sequel to *Julie of the Wolves*. Then, read *Julie's Wolf Pack*, the third book in the Julie series by Jean Craighead George.

- **Be an activist:** Jean Craighead George takes pride in the fact that she petitions for the safety and security of the environment. Help save endangered species of wolves and other animals around the world. Check out the following nonprofit organizations to find out what you can do to help these magnificent animals:

Defenders of Wildlife
  www.defenders.org/wupdate.html
U.S. Fish and Wildlife Service, Division of Endangered Species
  www.fws.gov
Wildlife Conservation Society
  www.wcs.org
Wolf Education and Research Center
  www.wolfcenter.org
World Wildlife Fund
  www.panda.org

Related Reading

Other books in the *Julie of the Wolves* series by Jean Craighead George

Julie (1994)

Julie's Wolf Pack (1997)

Other books by Jean Craighead George

Acorn Pancakes & Dandelion Salad and 38 Other Wild Recipes (1995)

Animals Who Have Won Our Hearts (1994)

The Big Book for Our Planet (1993)

The Case of the Missing Cutthroats: An Ecological Mystery (1996)

Cliff Hanger (2002)

The Cry of the Crow: A Novel (1980)

Dear Katie, The Volcano Is a Girl (1998)

Dear Rebecca, Winter Is Here (1993)

Dipper of Copper Creek (1956)

Elephant Walk (1998)

Everglades (1995)

Everglades Wildguide (1972)

The Fire Bug Connection (1993)

The First Thanksgiving (1993)

Frightful's Mountain (2001)

Giraffe Trouble (1998)

The Gorilla Gang (1999)

The Grizzly Bear with the Golden Ears (1982)

Hook a Fish, Catch a Mountain (1975)

How to Talk to Your Cat (1986)

How to Talk to Your Dog (1986)

Look to the North: A Wolf Puppy Diary (1997)

The Missing 'Gator of Gumbo Limbo (1992)

My Side of the Mountain (1959)

Nutik and Amaroq Play Ball (2001)

Nutik, the Wolf Pup (2001)

One Day in the Desert (1983)

One Day in the Tropical Rain Forest (1990)

One Day in the Woods (1988)

On the Far Side of the Mountain (1990)

Rhino Romp (1998)

Shark Beneath the Reef (1989)

Snow Bear (1999)

The Summer of the Falcon (1962)

The Talking Earth (1983)

The Tarantula in My Purse: And 172 Other Wild Pets (1997)

There's an Owl in the Shower (1995)

To Climb a Waterfall (1995)

Tree Castle Island (2002)

Vulpes the Red Fox (1948)

Water Sky (1987)

Who Really Killed Cock Robin? An Ecological Mystery (1991)

The Wounded Wolf (1978)

Movie based on Jean Craighead George's book

My Side of the Mountain (1969)

Books about wolves—fiction

The Call of the Wild by Jack London

Never Cry Wolf by Farley Mowat

White Fang by Jack London

Books about wolves—nonfiction

Journey of the Red Wolf by Roland Smith

When the Wolves Return by Ron Hirschi

Wolves by Seymour Simon

Books about survival—fiction

Brian's Winter by Gary Paulsen

The Cay by Theodore Taylor

Hatchet by Gary Paulsen

Nory Ryan's Song by Patricia Reilly Giff

The Sign of the Beaver by Elizabeth George Speare

Bibliography

Books

George, Jean Craighead. *Julie of the Wolves*. New York: HarperCollins, 1974.

Newspapers and magazines

Authors & Artists for Young Adults. Volume 8, 1992, pp. 61–72.
Children's Literature Review. Volume 1, 1976, pp. 90–91.
Contemporary Authors. Volume 25, 1989, pp. 156–158.
Hit List 2: Frequently Challenged Books for Children. 2002, pp. 19–20.
Writers for Young Adults. Volume 2, 1997, pp. 47–57.

Web sites

Alaskan.com: http://alaskan.com/docs/eskimo.html
Bookpage, First person interview, "Jean Craighead George searches for paradise in the swamp."
www.bookpage.com/0205bp/jean_craighead_george.html
Children's Book Council:
www.cbcbooks.org/html/jean_craighead_george.html
Christian Science Monitor. "Talking with Wolves, Then Writing About Them." September 25, 1997.: http://search.csmonitor.com/durable/1997/09/25/feat/books.3.html
Educational Paperback Association:
www.edupaperback.org/showauth.cfm?authid=29
Official Jean Craighead George Web site:
www.jeancraigheadgeorge.com